Wally jumped from bed early one Saturday morning. He looked around and realized he couldn't see!

"Mama! Papa!" He called as he stumbled from his room.

"Oh my!" Said papa.
"Your hair grew
inches overnight!
This is most unusual."

Grandma Polly
arrived just as they
were wondering how
this happened.

"Goodness gracious! This is peculiar. Just yesterday you had short hair!"

"I like it!" Wally giggled as Ollie sniffed him—just to make sure that it really was Wally underneath all that hair.

"We need to get you a haircut right away." Mama spoke as she put Wally into the stroller.

"A little trim here, a little cut there." Said the hairdresser as she quickly worked her magic.

But as soon as she finished...
Whoosh! Wally's hair grew back
even longer than before!

Everyone in the salon
stared at and were
amazed by what they saw.

10

"This is not normal." Barked Ollie, looking nervous.

Grandma Polly bent down to inspect his locks. "I've never heard of this before! We need to find someone who can help. I think I might know just the person!"

Papa, excitedly shouted, "We
must find a way to fix this.
Lead the way, Grandma!"

They ventured into the forest, up a winding hill and over a rushing river before they came to the person Grandma Polly had mentioned.

A kind looking old lady came
out of a door on the side of a
tree. "I've been waiting for you."
She spoke.

"I am Willow Winsington, but you may call me Madame Willow."

"I believe my brother, Sir William Winsington is behind this! Several people have come to me in the last few days asking why their hair is so long. He likes to play games and trick people by making their hair grow!"

"That must be it!" Shouted Wally. "Last night I had short hair, and now it just keeps growing!"

"I do not know how he is doing this. You'll have to find him and ask him to stop. But be warned, he will only do as you ask if you do something very silly and make him laugh!"

Wally looked at his family
and smiled. "I think we can
find a way!"

Everyone thanked Madame Willow and marched towards the house of Sir William.

Sir William Winsington didn't live in a tree as his sister did, but instead, in a cave!

Wally and his family knocked on the side of the cave, hoping to be let in.

"Who's there?" Shouted a voice from inside. Wally thought for a moment before answering with a knock-knock joke!

"Comb!" Said Wally.
"Comb who?"
"Can we comb in? I really
need a haircut!"

Nobody heard anything from inside the cave for several seconds, and then...

"Hahaha! That's the funniest joke I've ever heard!" Sir William said as he opened the door to the cave.

"Ah! You must be one of the people that used my new miracle shampoo! How do you like it?"

"I think my hair is pretty stylish, but I'm having a hard time seeing!" Wally responded.

"It was the shampoo?! We did just buy some at the store." Remarked Papa. "Could you make it a little less strong? It works too well!"

"Since you made me laugh with your joke, I will grant your request." Said Sir William, and with a quick phone call, the recipe to his shampoo had been changed to a less potent formula.

Wally and his family hurried home to enjoy the rest of their Saturday, knowing that Wally's hair would soon be the perfect length once again.

Check out another book in The Adventures of Wally, Ollie and Polly series!